book
This ~~Mess~~ belongs to

With love, as always, for Eilidh, who is still my little Pinkie even though she's 22 xxx — CS

Dedicated to my lovely mother Vivienne — FM

Special thanks to Anders for his fabulous design work — LDB

Published by Little Door Books 2021
This edition published 2021

ISBN: 978-1-9162054-1-3

Text copyright © Chae Strathie 2021
Illustrations copyright ©·Francis Martin 2021

Design and layout by Anders Frang

Printed in Turkey.

A CIP catalogue record for this book is available from the British Library.

LITTLE DOOR BOOKS

mail@littledoorbooks.co.uk
www.littledoorbooks.co.uk
twitter: @littledoorbooks

Pinkie was **NOT** happy.

Mum and Dad had told her
she was going to get
a little brother.

But **SHE** was the littlest
one in the family, unless
you counted Alan the Goldfish.

That's why everyone called
her Pinkie, just like the titchiest
finger on her hand.

Mum said, "You'll always be our little Pinkie", but Pinkie **KNEW** what would happen when the baby came along.

"I'll probably be left behind at the seaside and get carried off by **EVIL SEAGULLS**."

"Or fall down a **HOLE** and drop out of the bottom of the world."

"Or be turned into a **STINKY RAT** by a wizard. All because of a **BABY!**"

It... was.... a...

DISASTER!

When Mum and Dad brought the baby home Pinkie said, "It looks funny and it's too **LOUD** and it smells of cabbage."

"That's what **YOU** were like when you were a baby," laughed Mum.

"No I **WASN'T!**" said Pinkie. "I was a lovely little sausage."

Then she made a face at the baby.

Dad said if she was nice
she would get a present.

Her present was
a cuddly monkey.

"What are you going to call
the monkey?" asked Mum.

"I'm calling it Boo!" said Pinkie,
and she showed it to the baby.

"BOO!"

She yelled.

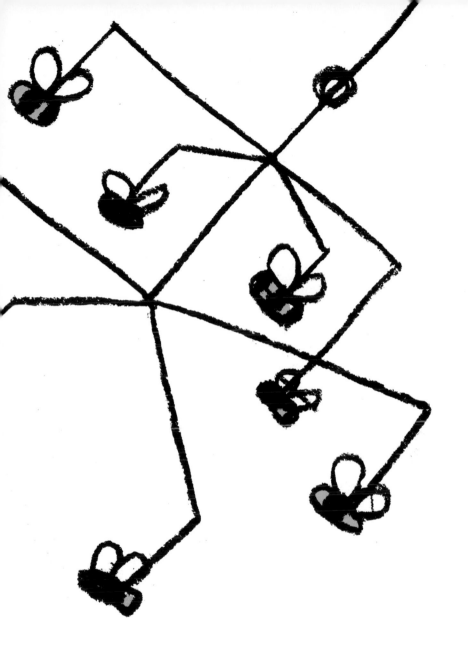

Mum and Dad didn't think
that was very funny.

Pinkie was sent to the garden
to play with Boo.

"What a lovely garden," said Boo.

"You can **TALK!**" gasped Pinkie.

"Of course I can talk," said Boo.

"Come with me," said Pinkie,
"I need to tell you all about the Baby Problem."

Pinkie told Boo about the baby getting **ALL** the attention.

"Being the littlest is **MY** job. What if Mum and Dad forget about me?"

That's when Boo had his first *SUPER-BRILLIANT* idea.

"We should pick Dad a lovely bunch of flowers
so he thinks you're **AMAZING**," said Boo.

So that's what they did.

"Now let's make Mum a milkshake
so she thinks you're **COOL**," said Boo.
"I love banana flavour, but we should
make an extra special one."

They used all the milk, one egg,
lots of tomato ketchup, a spoonful
of salt, fresh orange juice for health,
three fish fingers and thirteen
teabags because tea
was Mum's favourite.

Boo thought it would be a good idea if they
drew Mum and Dad some lovely pictures.

"We don't have any paper," said Pinkie.
"But we do have a nice, clean **WALL**," said Boo.

Pinkie and Boo used all the crayons.

"I hope Mum and Dad like them," said Pinkie.
"They're going to **LOVE** them," said Boo.

Boo was wrong.

"There are scribbles
EVERYWHERE!"
wailed Dad.

"Look at the **MESS**
of this kitchen!"
cried Mum.

"My **TULIPS!**"
sobbed Dad.

Mum and Dad looked at Pinkie.
Pinkie looked at Boo.
Boo didn't do anything.

"It was Boo's idea," Pinkie said.

Pinkie had to help scrub the walls.
Clean the kitchen. Tidy the flowerbed.

And after that she had to go to her room
To Think About What She Had Done.

"This plan did not
go well," sighed Pinkie.

"At least you got lots
of attention," said Boo.

Pinkie glared at him.

But then
Boo had
another
GREAT
idea.

"We have done
a drawing!"
said Pinkie.

Mum and Dad
looked worried.

But when Pinkie
showed them...

...they beamed the **BIGGEST** smiles ever.

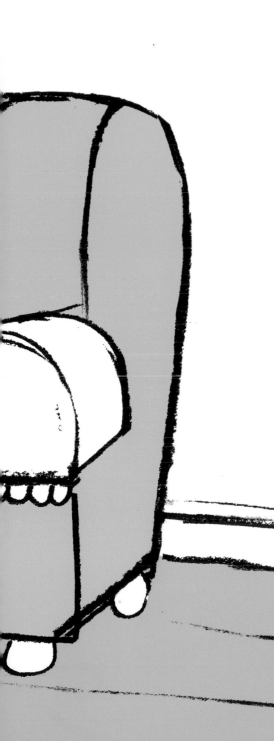

"Would you like a milkshake,
little Pinkie?" said Dad.

"One without tomato ketchup
and fish fingers," laughed Mum.

"Can it be banana flavour?"
asked Pinkie.

"And I'll need **TWO** straws, please..."